MEMOIRS OF CALCUTTA

The Little
GREEN WINDOW

MY WALK THROUGH THE MEMORY LANE

SOMREET BHATTACHARYA

ink Scribe

The Little Green Window

Publisher: Inkscribe Publishing Pvt. Ltd

ISBN Number: 978-1-966421-56-6

Contents

Preface

Set at a time before the world took the great economic leap, the Little Green Book narrates the author's walk through the memory lanes. The book paints a vivid tapestry of time, place, and emotion—intertwining the present with the past in a way that feels both nostalgic and deeply personal. The way you describe your balcony in Delhi as a portal to your childhood in South Calcutta is poetic, and the imagery of the Devil's tree, treepies, chipmunks, and sparrows creates a living, breathing ecosystem that mirrors the wild serenity of your childhood surroundings.

My bonding with my grandfather Dadu — a remarkable storyteller and a gentle soul—his shawl, cane stick, and baritone voice all come alive with the stories. His stories, whether real or imagined, shaped my sense of wonder and connection to nature and history. The tale of the tiger encounter, a trip to Odisha or the love for a girl who meets with a tragic end is especially gripping, and the transformation of Kumir-Pukur from a crocodile-inhabited pond to a wetland is a poignant reminder of how places evolve, yet memories remain rooted.

"We do not inherit the earth from our ancestors; we borrow it from our children."

– Ancient Indian proverb

The Little Forest on the Other Side

There is a Devil's tree outside my balcony where a pair of treepies have taken refuge, along with a family of chipmunks who have made my balcony a park for their daily strolls. I occasionally leave a bowl of water and some nuts early in the morning before their day begins to surprise them somewhat. They eat portions of the nuts and leave some for a pair of house sparrows or the crows that drop in.

On a lazy afternoon, this balcony at my house in Delhi acts as a time travel machine that takes me back to my childhood in the late 1980s to my study room at our house in south Calcutta. The name Kolkata was not coined back then, and I liked it more. The first-floor corner room had two large windows that opened onto an urban forest with a boundary wall. A large neem tree, a mango tree, a wood apple tree, a jamun and some betel nuts took up most of the sky space while the ground was full of weeds and at least a hundred smaller shrubs, which I couldn't identify.

A purple flower bloomed before the monsoon, and the forest was home to birds, chipmunks, civets, some reptiles and a pair of foxes, each of which had its own stories. Dadu, my grandfather, used to be the narrator of these stories. He made up most of them to keep me entertained, but I loved listening. He had light salt and pepper hair, wore a full-sleeve kurta and freshly ironed dhoti every day, and in winter, he would wrap a brown Kashmiri shawl. He carried a cane stick, which he had customised with help from a childhood friend so that it wouldn't slip if he walked on a marbled floor.

Our family was one of the area's oldest residents, who had bought tracts of land to build houses. The area used to be marshes earlier, but as the city grew in length and breadth, the civic authorities "reclaimed" the land from the marshes and sold it out. The locality had several houses since the 1950s and 60s - post

India's Independence. Dadu and his brothers had branched out from our ancestral home, a few hundred metres away and took up this space to erect a new house.

Dadu used to say that the plot where our house is situated had a large pond filled with saline water, a remnant of a lagoon that was a backwater of the Sundarbans, perhaps several hundred years ago. When Dadu was young, he recalled that a saltwater crocodile had made its way to the pond. It grew to around 14 feet, often taking cattle and poultry straying towards the pond as prey. Someone had finally shot the reptile with a double-barrel gun and used its skin for a pair of shoes.

While the magnificent reptile met with a tragic death, the area was renamed Kumir-Pukur (the pond of the crocodile) in its honour. The stories of these wild encounters always kept me hooked on Dadu. He was tall, had bright grey eyes and had a baritone voice. He used to speak slowly, narrating his stories to the minute details.

By the 80s, the pond became a wetland with hyacinth brimming the banks. The water was 'unusable' and was home to a few snakes and some waterfowl.

Dadu and I sat on the terrace on winter afternoons with a bowl of oranges. I used to peel them with my fingers while Dadu removed the seeds and handed them to me. The soft sunlight had a fudgy warmth, making it feel like a dream playing in live mode. Dadu used to sit on a reed mat cross-legged, and I sat beside him with our backs to the sunlight. He used to wrap his brown Kashmiri shawl around me and begin his stories about his encounters with civets, jungle cats and jackals and how he dealt with a tiger when visiting a friend in Sunderbans. Dadu was born in a quaint village in Burdwan, a district in West Bengal, in the early 1900s and had travelled to Calcutta with his parents when he was 24. His eyes brightened as he spoke about his childhood in the village. Dadu's father – my great-grandfather – had left the town and travelled to Calcutta with his family after the local zamindar forced him to give up his land after he protested against heavy taxation on the farmers. Back then, the colonial government imposed heavy tax rates on agricultural produce to compensate for the losses they incurred due to famines.

He was a priest at a temple built by the same zamindar. Dadu recalled that one fine morning at the temple, the zamindar came over and insulted him to the extent that he was forced to abandon the house and leave.

The family managed to reach Calcutta with a trunk full of essentials and rented a house near Kalighat, which was then the outer edge of the city during the colonial period. The family struggled to earn and finally set up a garments store at a south Calcutta market that still survives.

Dadu would recall that the house where he was born had a straw roof and mud walls. It was tucked between two palm trees where a pair of brahminy kites built their nests. He would recall how they shrieked through the day during monsoons. I always felt that he had left a part of his heart in the village when they abandoned the house. Later in life, Dadu went looking for a home, but someone razed it and set up an oil mill there.

I don't recall whether it was Dadu's narration or an inherent call from the wild; the imagination of a six-year-old me flew through the paddy fields and mangroves. The palm trees, thatched huts and dots of water bodies rushed through my mind, like watching the scenery outside a train window that runs past in fast forward in the opposite direction.

Dadu had stories about his encounters with tigers, bears and that of the super natural, I remember one of them where he was at a village near the Sunderbans. He was staying at a house of an acquaintance who laid a bed for him at the courtyard of their thatched hut on a hot summery night. "They had set up a mosquito ned for me to keep away the insects, but warned me to be alert about animals that often strayed into the courtyard," he said.

Around midnight, Dadu heard a scratching noise along the bush fence around the courtyard.

"A quick thinking saved my life", he recalled. He stepped out of the bed and climbed onto a wood apple tree nearby and after a few moments there was a huge male tiger that leapt over the fence and entered the courtyard. It went straight for the bed and ripped open mosquito net along with mattress tattering it to pieces.

"I still remember how it growled during that, while I was shaking in shock sitting on branch," he said. He recalled how he could smell the tiger from the branch he was sitting on.

The next day, Dadu bid goodbye to the family and returned back to Calcutta.

The roads in Calcutta used to fall silent in the afternoon as the city slipped into a post-lunch siesta. Dadu's stories played out in real time in my imagination.

Calcutta used to be different back then, I could relate to the stories looking at the tiny patch of forest beside our house. A Sunderbans forest must have looked the same. The shriek of a Brahminy kite or the calls of a flameback wookpecker would often drown the sound of a handful of cars and a few rickety buses that plied on the road near our house. Post noon, the city almost looked deserted.

I somehow miss the silence that resonated with the breeze rustling through the neem and mango leaves in the forest. For me, they sounded like voices asserting the stories that Dadu narrated.

In December, this forest turned mesmerising; the flowering plants used to bloom, and scores of birds swooped down to feast on bees and flies that feed on the flowers.

The pair of flameback woodpeckers, with their yellow back and red crest, nested on the betel nut trees and pecked on the bark throughout the day. A pair of civets also resided in the bark of the tree and often took their liberty to venture into our house. I used to wonder when they hit their beaks onto the hard surface of the tree. The monotonous peck sound would be accompanied by the chatter of a group of jungle babblers who parked themselves on the ruins of a wall with bare bricks that bordered the little patch of green. No one knew how and why a wall was erected in a patch of forest. The wall had thin bricks stuck together using lime, jaggery and sand.

The stories would be interspersed with the kuk-kuk sound of a coppersmith barbet, which announced the arrival of the cold season. I could never spot the bird, but the call brought back a feeling of unknown nostalgia about the quaint village tucked between palm trees.

A barbet occasionally visits the Devil's tree outside and sails my memories back to childhood, except that I miss the warmth of the brown shawl and the fudgy sunlight.

"When the last tree is cut, the last fish is caught, and the last river is polluted, we will realize we cannot eat money."

— Cree Native American Proverb

The Death of a Green

It hurts more when someone tears off a portion of your soul than a part of your body. I had learnt this in my pre-teens.

Days off from school in the later teens were mainly occupied with studies for the boards. The board exams in the 90s used to be a different experience, as there were stages of the test, each tougher than the previous ones. This was done to make the board exams look seemingly effortless for the candidates, though it rarely helped.

On lazy afternoons, I used to sit by the window facing the forest and let my mind sail through the Pacific Ocean with spinner dolphins and orcas as the pages of the maths textbook turned themselves with the soft breeze, hoping to draw my attention.

One such afternoon, the daydream broke with a hard, loud buzz. A group of men had entered the forest and started sawing down a giant mango tree. There was mayhem in the otherwise peaceful patch of green. Within a few minutes, the tree came crashing onto the forest floor, perhaps crushing a few birds and animals that had gathered in shock.

Over all these years, I connected to the forest with my soul, a part of which tore off. I shouted back at the men, asking them to stop, but they paid little heed. I ran to the terrace, asking why this sudden onslaught, and learnt that the patch of land was sold to a realtor for constructing a high-rise that would have a garden facing our house.

The crow that built its nest on the wood apple tree perched on my window ledge for the next few days, cawing in different tones as if raining curses on humanity. I would talk to him and try to reason out the acts of men, but he was pretty adept with them. Perhaps I was the only human he could get near without being shooed away to lodge his protest.

The forest was soon "cleared" of trees within a week, and trucks were rolled in to carry the portions of whatever was left behind by the bulldozers. The wood apple and the betel nut trees had fought bravely, refusing to fall despite being hit several times, but they were no match for chainsaws. Branches lay strewn across the forest floor, and a few nests of the birds that presumed the trees to be safe havens lay on the grass below the undergrowth. Their chicks were probably crushed under the wheels of the bulldozers.

A pair of house sparrows who had nestled in the wood apple tree outside my window had bravely swooped down on the men, chirping loudly, putting up a strong face in their losing the war.

A few days later, the chainsaws fell silent and left the once bustling forest deserted with a pall of gloom descending onto the walled compound. Among the broken branches, leaves and bird nests, a few jamuns fell on the ground, and a group of chipmunks tried to nibble up whatever they could find amongst them. The little forest they perhaps called home was gone in three days.

The remnants were soon cleared despite strong protests from a group of monitor lizards and a civet family who had hoped that the onslaught would end with the felling of the trees. Earthmovers were again called in to dig up the soil as if to punish them further for their "insubordination".

As a child, I could do little to lodge my protests; the voice of a pre-teenager perhaps seemed as feeble as that of the chipmunks. Dadu had called the plot owner and requested that he sell the plot of land to him so we could maintain the forest, but he flatly refused since he was probably making a fortune out of it after a realtor gave him a better deal. He used to respect Dadu and promised to set up a garden once a condominium was built on the plot. I could only look helplessly at the huge earthmovers clearing tree stumps and broken branches. The family of flameback woodpeckers would hit the panes of the earthmovers, hoping to push them back, but gave up after a few tries.

There was a void outside the window that faced the forest. I stopped looking outside, shifted my study table to another room, and, at times, avoided returning home from school during daylight hours to avoid looking at the empty plot of land.

This continued for a month until one monsoon afternoon when I decided to return to the bed in my study room. It filled up a corner and was cosy for a siesta. The chirping of two house sparrows awakened me - a couple that had entered through the window and kept flying in and out of a bookshelf with some ancient hardbound books neatly stacked. The couple seemed quite busy and were perfectly unfazed by my presence, even after I woke up and sat on the bed.

They carried twigs, hay strands, cotton and some cloth in their beaks and left them behind the hardbound books. This went on for days. I would never shut the windows so they could fly in and out, and I even left some water on the windowsill in case they needed some. We never used to run the fan in the room to avoid them being hit in case they flew too close.

A week later, the sparrows built a neat nest with the books and were busy starting a new family. Dadu was initially apprehensive about it, but later insisted that I don't pay much attention to the sparrows in case they feel "awkward" and stop returning.

A few weeks later, I could hear squeals from behind the books, indicating their new family. My job was to ensure the parents got enough passes to fly in and out for food. I had once tried peeping in, but shrieking protests from the parent sparrows prevented me from going nearby.

I felt a sense of belonging to the sparrow family, who had learnt to trust me with their chicks. Sometimes, both parents would leave the chicks unattended, knowing I would be there to protect them. Every time they returned, I would get a short thank you chirp as they perched on the grille before flying in behind the book stack. I would return from school quickly to look after the chicks, assuming the parent sparrows must have been tired. Dadu used to fill my place until I arrived, watching our new family members. He would debrief me on what transpired during the day while I was at school.

He used to say, "Dadubhai, it is now our duty to keep their family safe so that someone would look after ours when we need them. That is how the world runs. We watch each other's backs," he said.

One afternoon, I returned from school and found Dadu sitting on a chair with a gamcha on his shoulder. His hands were on his chest, and his eyes were red. He looked at me and smiled, saying he had a close shave with someone but managed to push him back. I was curious and kept asking him who it was, but my mother dissuaded me from asking further questions.

That evening, Dadu again fell ill and had to be shifted to a hospital in an ambulance. As his stretcher was being pushed into the vehicle, he caught a glimpse of my eye, winked and feebly lifted his hand for a goodbye. When I got closer to him, he mumbled, "Always look after the family while I am gone. I will perhaps return to ask you about how they are".

He never returned after that. Early the following day, the doctors declared that he had suffered two massive heart attacks. Later, the doctors mentioned that during his brief stay at the hospital, he was going through a delirium, during which he spoke about a group of sparrows and his home, a hut between two palm trees where a family of brahminy kites nested. My eyes swelled as I imagined him walking back wearing a white dhoti-kurta and his favourite cane stick.

I don't remember what happened to the sparrows and their chicks, but today, as I sit by my balcony in the bustling Delhi neighbourhood, I notice a pair of sparrows chirping around my chair. At first, I was amused by the couple's presence since Delhi doesn't see much of them, but they now seem to have adopted me, perhaps as a return favour.

"Curiosity is the wick in the candle of learning."

— William Arthur Ward

To Tell the Cat

Something peculiar happened when Dadu passed away: I returned home before 6 pm, but now the rule only existed in my head. The empty house no longer reprimanded me, yet I obeyed Dadu's invisible watchful eye, a habit I couldn't shake.

Afternoons stretched like chewing gum—sticky, endless, and slightly tasteless. I lounged on the terrace, chasing kites that seemed to taunt me, whispering secrets to the wind as they soared. Without Dadu's booming voice telling me tales of palm trees and civets, I started telling myself stories loudly and often with absurd plots involving heroic squirrels and philosophising coconuts.

The reed mat on which Dadu and I once sat was undergoing an existential crisis. By the next monsoon, it had given up on cohesion, shedding reeds like an overwhelmed hairbrush. I attempted surgery with tiny strings, only for them to sigh dramatically and snap. Somewhere, I imagined Dadu chuckling, amused at my pitiful attempts.

One day, treasure hunting in Dadu's belongings, I struck gold—or rather, paisa. A velvet pouch with coins gleamed at me, accompanied by a note: "This is what I am leaving for you to cherish." Rs 75! That was practically a kingdom's fortune in 1990s kid currency.

I soon claimed Dadu's puja attic as my secret sanctuary, though his books remained off-limits. He had forbidden me from touching them, saying they were meant for me "when I grew up." But when, exactly, did that happen? I decided the time was now. The reward was a gold-framed spectacle set (which made me look like a lost librarian), an encyclopedia older than all my ancestors combined, and a mechanical watch proudly proclaiming its "17 jewels." I wasn't sure where the jewels were, but I felt richer just owning them.

Then, the cat arrived.

She clambered up the rainwater pipe, dishevelled and furious at the universe, bleeding from her left shoulder but glaring at me like I was responsible. I lifted her carefully, nursing her wounds with an ancient handkerchief from Dadu's things—because if ghosts haunted heirlooms, I figured this particular ghost would be friendly.

The basket meant for puja flowers became her makeshift home, and she adapted quickly to a life of clandestine luxury. I fed her milk and bread, despite her apparent lack of gratitude. When she started sneaking out, scavenging food elsewhere, I realised I was merely her backup plan. Yet, she always returned at night, curling into her basket as if it were the throne of a tiny ruler.

Everything was smooth until one fateful Sunday.

The prayer ceremony for Dadu was held in the attic puja room, and the cat had to be hidden. She was under strict instructions to remain silent, but she did not listen.

As solemn chants filled the room, the cat decided it was the perfect time to perform an interpretive dance with the basket. She dramatically nudged her makeshift home to the centre, where offerings lay. The pandit froze mid-chant, believing his words had summoned supernatural forces. My mother screamed something about snakes. Then, with cinematic flair, two white paws emerged, grabbing a sweet meant for the gods, leaving a trail of chaos thereafter. Puja utensils were flying, flowers scattered, diyas tumbled and whatnot.

A courtroom was convened within minutes of this disaster. I was put on trial by all 11 members of my family, charged with harbouring a feline fugitive and disturbing sacred rituals. The sentence? My access to the attic was revoked. I, the former king of forgotten books and ancient coins, was overthrown after a few spanks on my back from Maa; there was punishment for solving thirty sums every afternoon before I could step out to play.

Years later, on a trip home to Calcutta, I found the keys to the abandoned attic. The lock was rusty, the books speckled with termite holes, and the reed mat practically skeletal. I stood there, a trespasser in an era where imagination ruled, eyes misting with memories.

A slight sound snapped me out of it—a tiny mew.

I turned in time to see a white tail disappear behind the almirah. I glanced at Dadu's smiling photograph, covered in dust yet somehow sparkling, and whispered, "Well played, old man." Then, locking the room, I stepped out.

"Traveling in the company of those we love is home in motion."

— Leigh Hunt

The Great Family Trip

My maternal family was large, with my mother's cousins living in the same vicinity in a town beside the Hooghly River near Calcutta. As a child, I was always awed by their extraordinary ability to plan extravagant family trips at the drop of a hat.

One winter evening, my mother and her cousins huddled together, reminiscing about their childhood in Puri. Before I knew it, the huddle had transformed into a plan for an overnight trip to Puri, one of the four holiest temples of India on the coast of the Bay of Bengal. This was back in 1996, and planning a trip of this scale required the precision of a mini travel company. Yet, within a few hours, train tickets were "arranged" through a travel agent, and the group was ready to set off.

I was always amazed by my family's ability to embark on trips with no clear plan, something I have perhaps inherited. According to them, "it all runs in the blood." The journey to Puri was somewhat mandatory for my mother's family, who had to pay obeisance every few years to Lord Jagannath, the presiding deity of the temple town.

It was about 9 p.m. when my parents agreed to join these trips. My maternal uncle, two of my aunts, and their families formed the core group, making up to a dozen members. My mother's cousins and their families joined them—another dozen people. Responsibilities were distributed between packing bags, cooking dinner, and coordinating with those travelling from different parts of Calcutta so that everyone converged at Howrah station, the iconic railway station built by the colonials when the city served as their capital.

In the 1980s and 90s, pre-liberalised India, travel in an air-conditioned compartment of the Indian Railways was considered a luxury. Distances like the ones between Calcutta and Bhubaneswar were usually travelled in a "general coach" or the non-air-conditioned ones with grilled windows, creaking seats, and the soothing rattle of the wheels on the rail tracks, which almost worked like a lullaby on overnight travellers.

The 24-member entourage boarded the Dhauli Express from Howrah station around midnight, securing almost half a compartment. Dinner, packed in tiffin boxes, was opened an hour later, and by 1 am, the train's sweet rattling, coupled with the compartment's gentle movement, lulled everyone to sleep. The train reached Bhubaneswar early the next morning after crossing the Mahanadi, and the family was ready almost instantly to commence the next phase of the trip. The journey was usually accompanied by singing and joking about the goof-ups made during the planning phases.

A bus was arranged with the help of a local tour operator, who was somehow less "professional" and had more heart back then. The driver agreed to travel three hours to Puri in the dead of night only if we fed him "luchi and aloo sabzi" the following day.

By the time we reached the then quaint town of Puri, it was snoring asleep except for the incessant sound of the sea crashing against the shore. The house we were to stay in was named "Sukh Sagar" and belonged to a distant relative of my masi's in-laws. It seemed to have been locked ever since the British left India. A massive iron-grilled gate across a huge lawn opened onto a near-dilapidated mansion with termite-infested wooden doors and windows. The entrance even had a portico that hung to one side, and everything else was shrouded in darkness. The said "relative" who lived in Baroda had graciously informed the caretaker to "attend" to us.

After much enquiry, through the broken doors, the old caretaker, with wrinkled eyes and thin arms carrying a candle, appeared at the main entrance after some of my uncles managed to push open the creaking main gate and enter the compound. The caretaker agreed to open up the three massive rooms on the first floor since the other ten rooms in the mansion had been locked since the 1960s.

The house was massive, with a checkered marble and granite floor verandah running along the rooms till the end. It had five rooms on the first floor and five on the ground floor. The caretaker claimed to occupy one of the ground-floor rooms, but we never saw him after he opened the rooms for us. The verandah opened onto the sea on one side and a plot of land on the other, which used to be a garden. There was a massive sculpture of a cherub with wings that hung from one of the parapets of the terrace.

All three rooms had huge beds, with at least five or six people fitting into each. One had to climb up onto the bed using a flight of four wooden stairs. The family had a quick dinner with some leftover food, and we were off to sleep after the long road journey. The swishing of the sea waves at a distance worked as a lullaby.

The following day brought a surprise. As we were about to leave for a sightseeing tour, someone informed us that the house had been abandoned in the early 1980s and had never had a caretaker. There was a collective gasp as some of my aunts recalled imagining apparitions and ghosts soon after this news dropped over a cup of tea prepared by my mother. Faces turned pale, and plans were afoot to pack our luggage and shift to a hotel, though only two hotels existed back then.

My father and a couple of uncles soon discovered that the man who had opened the door for us was a thief who had entered the house and unlocked three doors to look for valuables. When he decided to leave, our platoon had already reached the house and started calling out for people. The thief decided to play smart, pose as the caretaker, and open the doors before fleeing.

Though my mother and some of the aunts raised safety concerns later in the day, the family felt dejected being outsmarted by the thief. Nothing went missing from the house, as far as we could take stock of. The episode left the trip etched in my memory since that was the last time the family travelled together and perhaps because it was filled with events which the family or whatever is left of it now keeps reminiscting.

One of my uncles, who took extra care of his health to be precise decided to play a game of volleyball in chest deep sea water with the rest of us. The fairly big family meant, a fairly big team on each side – almost a crowd.

The game went well for the first few minutes but disaster struck thereafter, the healthy uncle, decided to show his skills and spot jumped on one of the volleys to send it back and eventually landed on the toe of an another uncle that emitted a crack sound.

He reeled in pain letting out whimpers and howls from the pain. He was dragged out of the water and rushed to a clinic nearby where doctors advised him a bed rest for the next one month due to a fracture. Our weeklong trip thus got extended to a month in the process.

Baba took this opportunity to take me on road trips around Odisha – the roads stretched endlessly before us, winding through hills, forests, and sleepy villages. I was just a child then, but those journeys with Baba etched themselves into the deepest corners of my memory. Road trips weren't common for families like ours, but Baba was never one to follow the ordinary path.

He was a quiet man with a mind full of maps and stories, shaped by books he borrowed from libraries across Calcutta during his college days. He had never left the country, but he had traveled the world through pages — tracing rivers, climbing mountains, and walking through ancient cities in his imagination. And now, he wanted me to see the world with my own eyes.

We stopped by the roadside to collect slate sheets from the Eastern Ghats, their surfaces cool and smooth in our hands. We trekked up nameless hills, watching birds dart through the trees and listening to the rustle of unseen animals. Baba would crouch beside me, pointing out the shape of a leaf or the call of a bird, his voice filled with quiet excitement.

One morning, we stood together on an empty sea beach, the sky still blushing with the first light of dawn. The waves whispered secrets to the shore as Baba explained how ships once set their course by the rising sun.

"I always want you to be the explorer," he said, his eyes on the horizon. "Ask questions about things you don't know. That will make you humble, as you see how diverse the world is."

His words stayed with me, echoing louder with each passing year.

That trip, Baba took exactly 36 photographs — the limit of a single 35mm film reel in his beloved National Panasonic camera. Each photo was a frozen moment: fisherwomen in vibrant sarees balancing baskets of fish, our family laughing as we played water volleyball in the sea, and the waves glowing with phosphorus under the moonlight. Every face in those pictures beamed with joy, lit by the wonder of discovery.

Those photographs now rest in an old album, their edges worn, their colors faded. But the memories they hold — of a father who saw the world as a place of endless questions and quiet marvels — remain vivid.

And every time I set out on a new journey, I carry a part of Baba with me — the first explorer I ever knew.

While sifting through many old documents a few days ago, I stumbled upon the album with a red jacket around it. The photos in it were stained due to their age. In one of the photos, the group stood on the sand with the Bay of Bengal behind them. Only five of the 23 members have now remained. My throat choked as I turned the pages. I could hear the swishing waves on the vast Sukh Sagar bed.

"Throw your dreams into space like a kite, and you do not know what it will bring back — a new life, a new friend, a new love, a new country."

— Anaïs Nin

The Perfect Manjha

Back in the 90s, Calcutta had a secret season. It wasn't just monsoon—it was kite season. The skies turned into a circus of colours, and rooftops became kingdoms. Every boy and girl with a spool of string thought they were kings and queens of the clouds.

Kite flying wasn't just a game. It was a full-blown tradition. The wind would whisper secrets in July and August, and we'd listen. The air smelled of wet earth, old rooftops, and ambition. We didn't just fly kites—we sent them into battle. The goal? Cut the other fellow's string and watch his kite tumble like a wounded bird. Then run like mad to catch it before someone else does.

The kite shops were tiny treasure caves. You could buy a kite for fifty paise, but the real magic was in the gossip. The shopkeeper always had a story—about a boy who once flew a kite so high it touched a cloud, or a manjha so sharp it could slice through five strings in one go. We believed every word.

Money was tight, so we made do. We patched up old kites, borrowed string, and sometimes made our own glue from flour and water. The rooftops were our laboratories. We tested wind, argued about angles, and shouted instructions like generals in war.

And oh, the joy of a good breeze! You'd feel it in your bones. The kite would rise, tug at the string, and suddenly, you weren't on a rooftop anymore—you were flying too.

Enter Chhotka—our uncle and reluctant supplier. He gifted us a spool of weaponised kite string, razor-sharp with embedded shards of glass. This, he declared, was the stuff of legends. Baba, an expert kite-flyer, taught us the sacred art of lifting our papery soldiers into battle, even when the wind refused to cooperate.

But Dadu had rules. He despised throwing money into the sky, metaphorically launching our savings into oblivion. He outlawed kite-buying altogether, forcing us to survive on scavenged kites. After his passing, the prohibition was lifted, but we still treated every kite purchase like a covert operation.

Then, the great manjha experiment was born.

Inspired by the street-side kite shops, my cousin and I decided that store-bought string was for amateurs. We were determined to concoct the deadliest manjha known to humanity—the kind that could slice through opponents' strings like a vengeful sword.

Step one: fundraising. We "borrowed" a five-rupee note from my mother's piggy bank, solemnly promising to return it once we became moguls.

Step two: ingredient sourcing. We secured tapioca seeds for glue (thanks to a friend's grocery connections) and hunted for glass shards like medieval alchemists. The true challenge? Jackal droppings. (Yes. This was an actual required ingredient (according to dubious sources).

Our search for glass was heroic. While raiding a friend's storeroom, I discovered two neon tubes. A deal was struck—he would trade his neon lights if we shared the majha with him later. Naturally, we agreed that if his parents noticed missing neon lights, we would deny everything.

The tubes were smuggled via terrace escape routes and carried into a graveyard. They were ceremoniously laid on the resting place of a WWI soldier before being smashed to oblivion. The fun fact that skipped our wildest imagination was that the neon light tubes explode when broken, because of the pressurised gas. Fun realisation: our hands were bleeding within seconds. Still, the mission was unstoppable.

Jackals were frequent spectators at our football matches near the cemetery. We had never interacted, but desperation outweighed our concern for wild canine diplomacy. Creeping near their pit, my cousin suddenly yelled, "FOUND SOMETHING!" and held up a glorious lump with unrestrained joy. It was ceremoniously wrapped in a sal leaf, transported with reverence, and brought to our terrace laboratory.

For reasons unknown, we boiled the ingredients in an earthen pot from Dadu's funeral—our choice of utensil. A makeshift oven was built from bricks "borrowed" from a nearby construction site, and the whole operation was stealthily conducted during siesta hours when no adult could foil our genius.

Soon, a pungent odour spread across the house—something between open sewage and unspeakable regret. But we had done it.

With the precision of ancient artisans, we coated the kite string, stretched it between poles, and stood back in awe. Our masterpiece needed a whole day to dry. The monsoon clouds loomed, but we refused to let fate intervene.

We barely slept, vibrating with excitement for our Independence Day debut. But fate had other plans.

A midnight storm destroyed everything. Poles were uprooted, and strings snapped. The entire concoction washed into oblivion. Dawn arrived, and we stood in silent mourning, staring at the wreckage of our ambitions. Kite season had chewed us up and spat us out, and the pain never really left.

Thirty years later, I stood on the same terrace, staring at an empty sky. No kites. No storms. No stolen neon lights. And I thought: kids these days are smart enough not to boil jackal droppings.

"Until one has loved an animal, a part of one's soul
remains unawakened."

— Anatole France

The Last of the Hanuman

Summer afternoons in Calcutta were quiet. After lunch, the whole city seemed to fall asleep. My family took long naps, and the streets outside were still. That was the best time for a little adventure.

I would climb up to the terrace with a piece of fruit in my hand. The neighbour's trees leaned over the wall, heavy with mangoes and rose apples. No one seemed to care for them, so I did. Sitting on the warm tiles, eating fruit in the sun, felt like a secret mission.

One afternoon, as I lay back chewing a rose apple, something tapped my forehead. I opened my eyes and froze. A large langur was sitting beside me. His grey coat shone in the sunlight, and his eyes were bright and curious. Then, without warning, he sat on my chest.

I didn't move. I didn't even breathe. He stretched out his hand, asking for my fruit. His fingers were soft, but I could see his sharp teeth. I gave him the apples, one by one. He ate slowly, dropping bits on the terrace and on me. When he was done, he leapt onto the mango tree, looked back once, and bared his teeth — as if to say, "Don't follow."

I lay there for a long time. Then I ran downstairs, too shaken to speak.

The next day, I went back to the terrace with a wicket stick. I wasn't sure what I would do with it, but it made me feel brave. The hot wind blew across the rooftop, and the tree swayed gently. I waited.

Then, I felt a soft touch on my palm.

He was back. Sitting quietly, watching me. I noticed he was missing a finger. His arms had old scars. His eyes looked tired. He was older than I thought — and alone. No troop, no family. Just a wanderer like me.

I ran inside, grabbed a guava, and gave it to him. He ate slowly, then left.

From that day on, he came every afternoon at three. I brought bananas, guavas, and biscuits. He ate them all, though he didn't like the same thing twice. Sometimes, he left little gifts — a leaf, a twig, a shiny stone — near the terrace door. If he came early, he would drop a pebble or bang the door to call me.

In those quiet afternoons, we became friends — a boy and a langur, both a little lonely, both looking for company.

But over the years, the langurs of Bengal began to disappear. Once, they were a common sight — leaping across rooftops, sitting on temple walls, or stealing fruit from roadside stalls. They were part of the city's rhythm, wild yet familiar. But as the trees vanished and buildings rose, the langurs lost their homes. Their troops scattered. Some moved deeper into the forests. Others, like my friend, wandered alone.

Now, it's rare to see a grey langur in Calcutta. The rooftops are quieter. The trees are fewer. And the afternoons, though still hot and still, feel a little emptier.

Then, one afternoon, Maa found us. I thought the langur would run, but he didn't. He sat calmly on the terrace floor, staring at her. Maa froze, surprised by his sad eyes. She didn't shout. Instead, she walked back inside and returned with a handful of biscuits.

After that, she became part of our quiet meetings. Every day, she reminded me to go upstairs and feed him. Sometimes, she'd sit with us, watching quietly as he ate. It felt like our little world had grown — still gentle, still silent, but now with one more heart in it.

But one afternoon, he didn't come.

I waited for hours. I checked the rooftops, searched the trees, called his name softly. But there was no sign of him. The terrace felt emptier than ever.

Days turned into weeks.

Then, a neighbour found a dead langur in his storeroom. He had a missing toe.

I never saw the body. I didn't want to. I preferred to remember him as he was — sitting beside me on the warm tiles, reaching out for fruit with his soft hands, leaving little gifts of leaves and stones by the door.

Sometimes, when the wind rustles the mango tree, I still look up, hoping to see a flash of grey fur or hear the soft thud of a pebble on the terrace floor. But I know he's gone.

And yet, in those quiet summer afternoons, he gave me something I'll never forget — a friendship that needed no words, and a memory that still sits gently in my heart. While, some part of me refused to believe it was him. I kept hoping he would come back.

Years later, I visited the banks of the Ganga near Haridwar. I felt a tug on my palm as I stood there, looking at the water.

I turned.

Bushy brows. Familiar eyes. A soft, expectant hand.

A warm feeling spread through me.

I reached into my pocket and gave him some nuts.

He sat beside me, leaning against my foot, eating slowly. He had an injured toe and the same dewy eyes.

Nothing had changed, like we had never parted, and maybe, we never had.

"Enjoy the little things in life, for one day you may look back and realize they were the big things."

— Robert Brault

The Bandh Games

Bandhs and general strikes were a part of our daily lives in Calcutta in the 1990s. Some irate politician would call a bandh, meaning a complete shutdown, at the drop of a hat to gain a bit of political mileage or, at times, just for fun. Often, these bandhs came suddenly, which meant schools had to send students home early, and office-goers had to leave to avoid being "harassed" by the minions of the political party. The already slow-moving city slowed down even more, mainly for a few days.

While the city creaked to a halt, a group of us took to the streets for a game of football or cricket, depending on the season. Mr Sachin Tendulkar or Diego Maradona, who were no less than gods to us, would have been proud of our dedication to their respective games.

The roads, main thoroughfares, or crossings turned into mini stadiums, with people gathering on the footpaths and road dividers to cheer or even place bets on the winning and losing sides if the game turned intense. I remember once when bets rose to Rs 100 and a pot of roshogolla for the winning team, which was more than enough motivation.

The games began sharp at 10 a.m., with stumps or goalposts set up at "internationally" set distances and teams chosen based on the locality the players lived in. Perhaps the political parties that called for the bandhs didn't mind, as the shutdowns had such "productive" engagements.

I remember one such football match between us and a group of "footballers" who played with a second-division football club and had even played a few international matches. Their team couldn't return to their destination due to the bandh and decided to compete against us at one of the major road crossings in south Calcutta. Goalposts were made using bamboo poles, and a set of tram lines acted as "field markers." A referee who had conducted a Mohun

Bagan-East Bengal derby in the 1980s agreed to do it for us, pro bono.

It was a hot summer morning, and our entire locality–para in Bangla rose to the occasion." The pride was at stake for them and their "home team." We were treated like kings for the day. Elderly uncles reached each of our homes the previous night, taking stock of our fitness and what strategy we would use to pin down the "away team" from the beginning.

Being one of the "coaches," Baba assured them of it. He even arranged for a team meeting early the following day over boiled eggs and milk (we were barred from having tea or fried fritters that day) so that everyone in the locality was assured of our high morale. It felt nothing short of a modern-day press conference.

The match would begin sharp at 10 a.m., and some concerned "local uncle" offered to sponsor our breakfast of bananas and buttered toast. We were even motivated by another family with a lunch of mutton curry and rice if we managed to win.

The match started with all the "FIFA-mandated formalities," which we had no idea about back then, except for a few elders who formed juries to set the rules. The ball was kept between the tram lines that acted as the centre line markers. The eleven-a-side teams even had jersey colours, with the away team wearing whites while we wore blue. Some were barefoot, while others wore canvas shoes against the other team's expensive sneakers.

This "handicap," as the uncles termed it, was somehow celebrated by them, as the narrative of an underdog team facing a superior opponent went around as a buzz. The "away team" even managed to muster supporters from the other localities we had defeated in a previous match—a year before this.

I used to play as a left centre midfielder, while my cousin Joy and a friend manned the flanks — not really the ones who dashed along the sidelines like wind, but some one who could hold off. The first three minutes of the match were uneventful, until I came face to face with the away team's striker. He was tall — six feet, maybe more — and built like a bamboo pole wrapped in muscle. He bolted toward me with the ball, and I knew I had to stop him before he reached the goal box.

I held my breath and ran to intercept. I slid in, my shin brushing against his leg. What followed was pain — sharp, blinding, like being struck by a bamboo staff. I tumbled, face-first, as he swerved and took the shot. From the ground, I heard the roar of the first goal from the opponent's crowd — boys on terraces, rooftops, even the local masjid, all cheering like it was the World Cup.

The locality uncles gasped in unison. I lay there, stunned, a tear rolling down my cheek — not just from the pain, but from the realisation that this team was built like a battalion. Eleven of them. All bolts of lightning.

The match went on. Three more goals followed before halftime, each one a long-range missile. We trudged back to our "camp" — a converted Calcutta Police kiosk with a bench and a broken fan. Baba stood there, arms crossed, moustache drooping in deep thought. I had just taken a bite of a banana when he stormed in.

"What are you doing here with a banana in your mouth while the team is in this state?" he thundered.

I froze, mid-chew. Joy and another player were already down to their underwear, trying to cool off. Baba's scolding echoed off the tin roof until an older locality uncle stepped in. He calmed Baba down and turned to the team with a plan.

He had noticed something — the away team's sneakers slipped on the tramlines and the smooth asphalt beside them. That was our opening.

The new strategy was simple: avoid direct confrontation. Keep to the flanks. Use the tramlines. Our players would pass the ball quickly to the wings, where Joy and the others could sprint freely. The away team, with their fancy shoes, couldn't keep up on the slippery surface.

It worked like magic.

Every time we charged, the ball flew to the flanks. The away team slipped, stumbled, and cursed. Our boys danced along the tramlines, cutting in just in time to shoot. Three goals in fifteen minutes. The crowd swelled — vegetable vendors, a cobbler, schoolboys, and uncles with radios tucked under their arms. Even the local police leaned out of their post to cheer.

The match ended in a draw. But to us, it felt like a win.

That evening, we were treated to mutton curry and rice. And the bandh called by a political party for the next day? Quietly called off — perhaps in celebration, or in silent surrender to the spirit of the game.

While Calcutta remains a city with its own pace, bandhs and gully football no longer happen. The grounds have now been converted to high rises, and the roads are now filled with parked cars. The city has changed its character over time, but the streets still tuck in a few memories here and there to cherish.

"Love never dies a natural death. It dies because we don't know how to replenish its source."

— Anaïs Nin

The Enchanting Hills

I had never been to Darjeeling until I had finished college. I wanted to earn a bit of pocket money, a big issue back in the day and took up the job of documenting the history of a school in Darjeeling. I had to stay there for several days, going through the books. The road to Darjeeling was treacherous back then if you were travelling post-monsoon. There would be landslides often, and the trekker vehicles that ferried passengers from Siliguri, the nearest town, would get stuck in the mud, requiring at least 3-4 people to push them out.

The lush green eastern Himalayas commanded a charm beyond words; tiny hamlets with white and pink houses dotted the dark green hills, often backdropped with grey clouds that often gathered and disappeared. Lush tea gardens, which produced the famous tea, brewed up an enchanting smell that often clung to the landscape. The school had a sprawling campus overlooking a tea garden in Mirik, a town way off Darjeeling. It had a mountain lake and a set of 10 − 12 houses that formed the entire populace of the town back in the early 2000s

There used to be electricity at night, but the days were mostly spent outside, soaking in the sun. I usually scanned through the books and rarely stepped out, but an occasional liberty to walk around the town, taking hikes up into the forests or sitting by the lake sketching the hills, mostly after lunch, was the only change I longed for.

On perhaps the second day of my lazing trip, I climbed downhill into one of the tea gardens. Someone mentioned that the smell of raw tea makes you feel ecstatic if you are there for a long time. I met Jigme, whose father used to work in the same school. He became a self-appointed guardian after he found me hiking in the forests one evening.

Jigme took a long stick with him as we climbed through the steeper slopes to reach the tea garden, as the motorable road would require a longer walk. I had never climbed down a steep hill and slipped a few times. Jigme laughed every time I did so. Though it had not rained in Darjeeling that year, the grounds used to be slippery due to the incessant dew.

After struggling with a few slips and slides, I managed to reach the comparatively flat ground at the tea garden and rested myself against a tree that looked like it had held onto the rest of the mountain. Jigm, who was behind me, was nowhere to be seen. I called out for him a few times, but he seemed to have disappeared altogether. I had heard him laugh when I had slipped the first few times, after which I recalled he had stopped responding, too. The first thought that crossed my mind was that I had lost Jigme on the way by taking a detour, and then he must have been looking for me on the other side of the hill. I quickly tried to climb back the way I came from, but slipped, and every time I fell, a chunk of loose soil from the mountains kept covering the little path that I took.

Soon, the path was under a mound of earth, blocking my way out.

I tried to climb over it, but found it too risky since the mound was loose enough. I was virtually stuck between a tree, which I believed held the mountain and a mound that refused to allow me to climb back. We had started by the afternoon, and it was already dark when I was stuck on finding my way back. The fun part about the daylight in the hills is that you might see the sunshine on a hill at a distance while you remain shrouded in darkness due to the shadow of the mountains behind you.

After trying a few times, I was about to give up when a soft hand held onto mine. I was startled at first. The hands were soft and warm, but firmly gripped my wrist. I looked up, and our eyes met. There was an instant connection, a spark that ignited something deep within me. At the end of the hall was a girl with the most beautiful doe-like eyes and long, black hair, loosely tied in a bun. She had a smile that had the warmth to melt a few chunks of snow from the hills nearby, and a tiny dimple on her cheek made her face glow. I couldn't help looking at her for a few minutes — that seemed like an eternity until she tugged at my wrist and pointed her eyes to a gap in the mound where I could place my foot and pull myself out while she stood. That moment, I knew my life would never be the same.

She was Ananya — her father, who used to be an Army colonel, owned a plot of land near Mirik, and their family had shifted there after he retired from service. I got to know all this later. I had never imagined that my embarrassing "rescue operation" would also lead me to come back to the same place again.

After climbing out of the "mess," I thanked Ananya, and she insisted that I would have to join her for a cup of coffee if I was genuinely thankful for her efforts. Though it had got late by then, I decided to participate in a tiny cafe that sold a fantastic cuppa, or that was what it seemed to be back then. Ananya spoke about her travails across the country and how she was into writing books, climbing mountains and reading about wildlife. She even offered to hand me a pair of binoculars if I wanted to join her for one of her butterfly expeditions. I showed her my sketches, which impressed her.

Ananya always had this habit of tugging my little finger whenever something exciting caught her eye. Her eyes would light up like fairy lights every time she spotted her favourite butterfly or a bird I could never quite identify. It was as if she had a magical connection with nature, and I was lucky enough to be part of her enchanting world.

I couldn't help but notice that Ananya smiled every time, the little dimple on her cheeks made her words ring at a distance. She wore a light jacket, a pair of trousers, and sneakers that she said her sister had got from the US. Ananya also had this assertive tone to her voice whenever she tried to impress something on someone. A breeze hit my face every time she looked at me, asking for something.

As the evening turned to night, I walked with Ananya to a crossing that led to her house and returned. Jigme found me on the way and scolded me like my mother would have if she had seen me in a pot of murk.

I met Ananya for the trip the next day and walked to the sunset point early the next morning. Jigme promised to join me in an hour. We walked with binoculars up the road, and Ananya introduced me to the flycatchers and passerines. She caught my arm every time I walked to the edge of the road with the binoculars to my eyes. She spoke about her hiking trips to the Valley of Flowers and then to Kashmir, where she had seen the Himalayan tahr.

We reached the sunset point before the sunlight broke out through the pine trees and stood there silently till the first rays hit the top of the mountain. Ananya wrapped her little finger around mine for a long time. A happy yet tingling feeling rolled down my neck. I looked at Ananya, and she smiled back at me; her eyes glistened, and the dimple on her left cheek made my heart skip a beat; there seemed to be a slow version of Annie's Song, by John Denver, playing at a distance. For a late teen, this feeling must be as soothing as a ray of warm sunshine on a cold, hilly morning—the petrichor from the dew from the previous day added to the melody.

It had started raining on our way back, as we sought shelter under the awning of the old café, I mustered the courage to confess my feelings. The rain drummed a steady rhythm on the tin roof, and the world outside blurred into a hazy dream.

"Ananya," I began, my voice trembling with emotion, "I've always felt something special between us. You make my world brighter."

She looked at me, her eyes reflecting the soft glow of the streetlights. "I've felt it too," she said, her voice barely above a whisper. "You bring a sense of wonder to my life."

There was a brief exchange of a few shy looks, after which Ananya decided to walk back along the way, and we walked to the sunset point. She glanced back a few times and disappeared behind a bend. I stared at her, and the raindrops never felt like that before.

At a time when there were no mobile phones, we usually waited for each other at the sunset point. We talked about school, plans, and plans ahead. Ananya wanted to be a pilot and fly an aeroplane.

It had almost become a routine for her to meet for a few hours during my work breaks at sunset or during morning walks, after which we could not contact each other unless we decided to walk up to the other's residence.

After a day-long search, I got Ananya her favourite book from a shop near Glennary's and decided to wait for her on the rickety bench at the sunset point, where we spent most of our time. It was the 15th of August, and the schools were closed. There was quite an excitement as the first surprise should always be special. I quickly finished my breakfast of two toasted breads, eggs, and cornflakes and rushed to the usual meeting point.

Clouds had again started gathering in the distance, the direction from which the sun rose. I quickly occupied our usual spot, brushed my hair with my fingers and kept a note ready for Ananya to appear. A thundercloud cracked at a distance, and I looked at my watch. It was already 8 am, she usually turned up by now, but Ananya didn't turn up that day. I kept looking down the path, but there was no sign of her. After nearly an hour, I heard a rustling of leaves on the road; my heart again skipped a beat. I hoped to see long, wavy hair loosely tied in a bun, but Jigme ran down the path. He was panting heavily.

"There is a landslide, and several cars have flown into the Teesta River. Ananya's family was there in one of the cars," he said after taking a few long gasps.

My heart seemed to have stopped momentarily, and I couldn't believe him at first. We ran up to the main road, and police vehicles and a taxi were rushing down the hills, a few others from the village were also rushing to the spot. The taxi driver, Pachen, offered me a lift if I was planning to head to the place, and, within a few minutes, we were on the river's edge. A significant portion of the road had caved into the river due to the landslide, and a few cars were hanging on the edge, stuck onto one of the barriers.

A few cars had also flown down the river and toppled against a rock nearby. I could not find the vehicle Ananya and her family must have been travelling in. Some eyewitnesses claimed that a few lighter cars had flown downstream, and their vehicle could be one of them.

The search and rescue teams were deployed within a few hours, and the vehicles stuck against the rock were lifted out. One search official said that efforts were being made to track the vehicles that had flown down the river. There were no signs of them until late evening, though. Some eyewitnesses assumed the survivors must have escaped, while others were apprehensive.

Jigme and I stood waiting for some news until late at night, but no one could tell us about the missing vehicles, and no one had seen them. I could not sleep that night, and the image of the cars kept haunting me. While I sat up, looking out the window at the full moon that appeared over the mountain ridge, Ananya seemed to be there several times when I tried to shut my eyes. I could see her smile.

The police arrived at Ananya's house the next morning looking for a family member. When they didn't find one, they approached the school that my grandfather attended and asked someone to identify a few bodies that were recovered from the mishap site. I felt weak in my knees with the very idea of seeing the bodies as Jigme and my grandfather left for the mortuary in Siliguri. Jigme promised to get back if he had "news". I waited eagerly through the day until they returned. Police had found the mangled remains of the car, but there were no bodies in it. The bodies that they found were not those of Ananya or anyone from her family.

A few days passed, and the rescue operation was finally called off with little hope of recovery. I was devastated all this while looking for closure to something that I had hoped would be a bright future. The world has turned topsy-turvy ever since. I had stopped going to the sunset point or even on the road which led to Ananya's house, mostly confining myself in the room at the school, reading books or studying, occasionally stepping out only to talk to Jigme till the day finally came when I had to head back to Calcutta.

I had to apply for admission to a master's course after that. In those days, you had to collect admission forms in person, fill them out, and submit them back to the college office for admission. There used to be queues outside the colleges at this time. I remember standing in one such queue outside a college in north Calcutta, sweating profusely, when a soft set of hairs brushed by my neck along with a familiar floral perfume that Ananya wore; I was startled and quickly turned and saw her wearing a white kurta and a blue skirt walking towards a crowd that had gathered to check for names on a list. I ran behind her, calling out her name, but she had disappeared by the time I could make my way through the crowd of students. I tried asking a few people, but no one had noticed her. I ran down the road towards a tram stop ahead, hoping she would head there, but there was no one. She seemed to have vanished as quickly as she came. I was sweating in the Calcutta heat, and felt a tear rolling down my cheeks.

Twenty years have passed since then, and I have never heard from anyone about Ananya, even Jigme, who claimed that their house in the hills was taken over by a builder now constructing a homestay there. I still wonder if it was a reality or an apparition that played out in my life.

"Sometimes you will never know the value of a
moment until it becomes a memory."

— Dr. Seuss

The Shushuks

Every summer, like clockwork, I was bundled off to my maternal grandmother's house for a fortnight of familial chaos and clandestine adventures. This wasn't just any house—it was Vishram Mandir, a grand old dame of a building perched on the edge of Calcutta, flirting with the Hooghly river like it had secrets to spill.

The house was a riot of red cemented floors, creaky doors, and mysterious rooms that only saw daylight during the summer holidays. Its columns were so ornate they looked like they were auditioning for a Mughal soap opera. Relatives would descend from all corners of the country, turning the place into a sort of Bengali Hogwarts reunion—minus the magic wands but with plenty of fish curry.

Now, legend had it that my great-great-great-grandfather (or some similarly moustachioed ancestor) had fought in the Boer War with the Afghans in Kandahar, earned a tidy sum, and bought the land from the Maharaja of Burdwan. Naturally, he built a house that looked like it could host a royal durbar and a cricket match at the same time.

But the real magic happened on the terrace. Sculptures of fairies lined the ledges, gazing wistfully at the river. My mother and her sisters, in their younger, more aquatic days, would dive off the terrace into the Hooghly like mermaids on a mission. I, of course, was too chicken to try, but I watched with wide-eyed wonder.

Afternoons were sacred. Post-lunch siestas were a Bengali ritual—windows shut, rooms turned into dark caves, and the entire family sprawled on the floor like a pack of snoring sardines. That was my cue. I'd sneak out through the back gate, barefoot and beaming, to the riverbank.

There, a flotilla of oar-boats bobbed lazily, tied together like gossiping aunties at a wedding. I'd hop from boat to boat, chatting with the boatmen who knew my entire family tree better than I did. My favourite was Karim Chacha, a wiry old man with a laugh like a kettle on the boil and stories that could outlast a monsoon.

Karim Chacha would often sit by the river, mending nets or smoothing the wooden ribs of a boat with his calloused hands. He wasn't a man of many words, but when he spoke, it was with the weight of memory.

He said he was born somewhere in East Bengal — perhaps Kumilla, though he wasn't sure anymore. "Before the country was cut up by the sahibs," he would say, his voice soft, almost apologetic. His father had rowed boats there too, ferrying people across the wide, muddy rivers that ran like veins through the land. Karim had learnt the craft from him — how to read the water, how to patch a hull, how to listen to the wind.

Chacha was in his forties when East Pakistan became Bangladesh. The war came like a storm — sudden, loud, and full of fire. He never spoke much about those days, but once, while fixing a broken oar, he told me in a low voice, "We were not wanted. Not here, not there."

He had stayed behind when others fled. His wife and two children had vanished during the chaos — taken, lost, or killed, he never knew. He searched for weeks, walking from village to village, asking, hoping. But the only thing he found was silence.

When he finally crossed the border into India, he carried nothing but a small cloth bag and a boatman's knife. He settled in a refugee camp near the river, where the land was soft and the water familiar. Over time, he built a small shack and began repairing boats again. People called him "Karim Chacha," and he became part of the para — a quiet man with sad eyes and strong hands.

Children liked him. He never scolded, never raised his voice. He would carve little wooden boats for them, and sometimes, if the river was calm, he'd take them out for a short ride. "The river remembers," he once told me. "It carries everything — joy, sorrow, even the names we forget."

Years passed. The war became a chapter in history books. But for Chacha, it was never over. It lived in the way he looked at the sky before it rained, in the way he folded his clothes with care, in the way he never locked his door — as if still waiting for someone to return.

One winter morning, we found his shack empty. The firewood was stacked neatly. His tools were in place. But Chacha was gone. Some said he had gone back across the border. Others believed he had walked into the river, the only place that had ever truly known him.

But I like to think he found peace — maybe in a quiet village by the water, where the boats still creak and the wind still sings the old songs of Bengal.

One sultry afternoon, he called me aboard and offered me a cup of tea—not your average cuppa, mind you, but one brewed from milk squeezed out of poppy seeds. Yes, *posto tea*. It tasted like dreams and rebellion. I fell asleep on his boat, lulled by boatmen's lullabies and the river's gentle rocking.

Then came the day of the Sushuk – the elusive Ganges river dolphin.

"Ever seen one?" Karim Chacha asked, eyes twinkling.

I shook my head, and before I knew it, we were adrift in the middle of the Hooghly. The boat bobbed like a cork, and then—plop!—a greyish blob emerged from the water and vanished again. "There!" he pointed. And there it was again—a Ganga river dolphin, shy and slippery, like a ghost with a sense of humour.

They weren't like the dolphins you see in glossy documentaries—no acrobatics or chirpy squeals. These were quiet, almost solemn creatures, with long, beak-like snouts and tiny eyes that seemed to squint at the world. They surfaced with a gentle sigh, like older men waking from a nap, and disappeared just as silently. The locals believed they were river spirits, guardians of the Hooghly, and some even said they could understand human sorrow.

Back then, they were a common sight. They'd glide through the water in pairs or threes, their bodies slicing through the river like ink strokes on a scroll. Sometimes, if you were lucky, you would even see the long snouts, sometimes for a few seconds and a blind head.

Now? Not so much.

Years later, I returned to that ghat. The boats had grown motors and bad tempers. The river was louder, angrier. No more *posto-tea*. No more fairy dives. No more Karim Chacha.

But sometimes, when the wind is just right and the river forgets to be modern, the dolphins still whisper to the fairies on the terrace. And somewhere, in a boat made of palm wood and memories, Karim Chacha is still playing cards, waiting for a curious child to ask about the Sushuk.

"Bonding is not measured by time spent together, but by the comfort you find in each other's presence."

— Unknown

The Leopard

After I finished college, I got a job as a junior teacher at a private school in Kalchini, a quiet town in North Bengal near the Buxa Tiger Reserve. The town was peaceful and beautiful, with hills in the distance and green paddy fields all around. Though a highway passed nearby, Kalchini felt far away from the busy world.

I lived in a small two-room house on the ground floor. It belonged to a colleague who lived upstairs with her husband. They gave me food in exchange for a small rent. The house had a lovely view, and when dark clouds gathered over the hills, it looked like a perfect picture.

Behind the house was a courtyard with a barbed wire fence covered in plants. My colleague warned me not to go there after dark.

"There are leopards that come looking for food," she said every night before going upstairs.

I never saw one, but deep down, I hoped I would. I spent my evenings reading books or listening to music. The village nearby would go quiet by 8 p.m., with everyone asleep.

One summer evening, as I read by the window, I felt a presence. I looked up—and there they were. Two glowing yellow eyes, still and curious, watching me through the glass. My heart raced. I stumbled off the bed, but the eyes didn't move. Slowly, a head appeared, ears twitching, and then the soft pattern of spots. A leopard.

I stepped closer, and just like that, it was gone— leaping over the fence and into the night. The moment was brief, but it stayed with me. I wanted to see it again.

So I began leaving small offerings—pieces of chicken, bits of chapati—outside the window. I told no one. Days passed. Then one evening, the eyes returned. This time, they seemed to recognize me. The leopard sniffed the air, its breath fogging the glass. I placed my hand on the pane, and for a moment, we were connected—two beings from different worlds, separated by a thin sheet of glass.

Then I noticed the door beside the window. It was unlocked. Slowly, I opened it just a little and made a soft sound. The leopard paused, alert but not afraid. I picked up a piece of chicken and held it out. It came closer, step by step, until it gently took the food from my hand. Then it walked to a corner of the courtyard and ate, calm and content. In that quiet moment, something changed. We were no longer strangers.

Over the weeks that followed, the leopard returned often. It would arrive at dusk, press its nose to the glass, and wait. I began to recognize its moods—the way its ears twitched when it was curious, the way it blinked slowly when it felt safe. I spoke to it in whispers, not expecting it to understand my words, but hoping it felt the warmth in my voice.

Sometimes, it would sit quietly while I read aloud, as if listening. Other times, it would nudge the window gently, asking for food or simply my presence. I began to feel its absence when it didn't come. It had become part of my life, a silent companion in the stillness of the hills.

One evening, it let me touch its whiskers. Another time, I rested my hand on its head, feeling the soft rise and fall of its breath. It trusted me. And I, in turn, felt a kind of love I had never known—pure, wordless, and wild. It was not the love of ownership or control, but of quiet understanding and mutual respect.

But love, like the seasons, changes.

The rains came slowly at first—soft, gentle, like a whisper. But soon, the sky opened up, and the hills began to cry. Day after day, the rivers grew louder, angrier. The green fields outside my window disappeared under water. Everything felt heavy, quiet, and sad.

And then... he stopped coming.

Every evening, I sat by the window, waiting. I looked for those glowing yellow eyes, for the soft sound of paws on wet ground. I waited for the breath on the glass, the gentle nudge, the quiet presence that had become part of my life. But the window stayed clear. The food I left remained untouched. The silence grew deeper.

I told myself he would come back. Maybe tomorrow. Maybe the day after. But deep down, I knew something was wrong.

One morning, after a long night of rain, I stepped into the courtyard. The air was cold. The ground was muddy. And then I saw it—a small patch of golden fur caught on the barbed wire fence. Wet. Still. Lifeless.

My heart broke.

I stood there for a long time, unable to move. The leopard—the one who had trusted me, who had come to me night after night—was gone. Taken by the flood, by the wild river that had swallowed the fields.

Since that day, the courtyard has never felt the same. The wind still moves the creepers. The rain still taps on the window. But now, every sound carries a memory.

I remember the way he looked at me, not with fear, but with quiet trust. I remember the warmth of his breath on the glass. The way he gently took food from my hand. The way he let me touch his whiskers, rest my hand on his head.

We never spoke a word. But we didn't need to.

It was a bond built on silence, on patience, on love. A love that didn't ask for anything. A love that simply was.

And though he is gone, I still feel him—in the wind, in the rain, in the quiet moments when the world holds its breath.

He was more than a wild animal. He was my friend.

www.ingramcontent.com/pod-product-compliance
Lightning Source LLC
Chambersburg PA
CBHW051929240626
47153CB00004B/1428